Sing, Sophie!

Written by
Dayle Ann Dodds

Illustrated by
Rosanne Litzinger

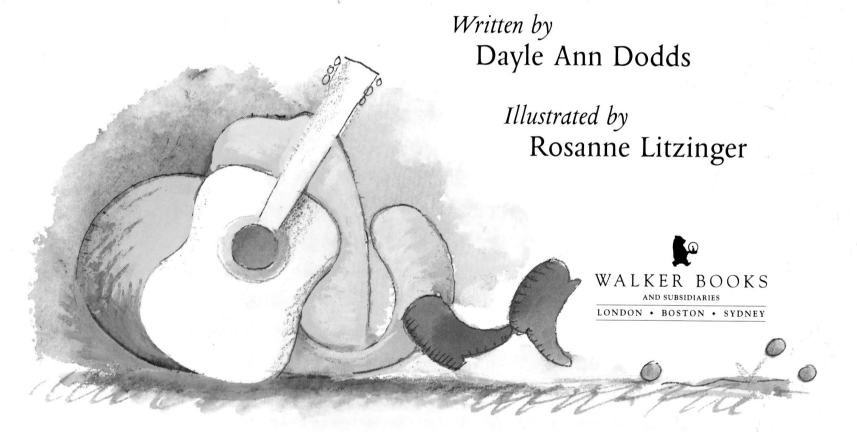

WALKER BOOKS
AND SUBSIDIARIES
LONDON • BOSTON • SYDNEY

Little Sophie Adams had a voice so big, folks claimed they could hear her from Corn County clear to the Western border.

"I *looooooove* to sing!" said Sophie, strumming her guitar.

"My dog's run off, my cat has fleas,
My fish won't swim, and I hate peas.
But I'm a cowgirl through and through,
Yippee-ky-yee!
Yippee-ky-yuu!"

"Mama, listen to my new song," said Sophie.
"It's hot, Sophie," said Mama. "And Baby
Jacob's trying to nap. Why don't you
share your singing with the birds?"

"*Aw, Mama.*" Sophie took her voice out into the garden. She strummed her guitar and sang out her song...

"My rooster won't crow, my hen won't lay,
My frog got warts and hopped away.
My legs are skinny,
my toes are fat,

"Sophie! You stop that bellowing right now!"
Sophie's older sister, Kate-Ellen, called. "With
this sticky heat and all your racket, my new
fluffy hairdo is fixin' to fall as flat as a flapjack!"

"Oh, *fiddle-faddle*!"
mumbled Sophie. "Doesn't
anyone want to hear my new song?"

At the creek she flopped down under a
shady laurel tree. Once again, Sophie
began strumming and singing…

"My coat is torn,
my shoes are wet,
My socks don't match,
my rat's upset.
My kite got stuck,
I ate a bug,
I spilled red cider
on the rug.

But I'm a cowgirl
tried and true,
Yippee-ky-yee!
Yippee-ky-yuu!"

"Sophie," said brother Willy.
"Can't you see I'm trying to fish?
Your caterwauling is scaring them
all away! Go somewhere else."

"Oh, *chicken feathers*!" Sophie said. "I've got a song in my heart and it *needs* to come out!"

Sophie leaned against the cool wall of the barn and strummed out a tune...

"My jokes are bad,
my riddles no good,
My hair never curls
the way that it should,

But I'm a cowgirl,
Yes-sir-ree!
Yippee-ky-yo!
Yippee-ky-yee!"

"Take your singing somewhere else, sweet pea," Sophie's papa called. "Old Betsy's getting fidgety in this heat and the milk pail's sitting empty."

"Oh, *goose grease!*" said Sophie. "Doesn't anyone want to hear me sing?"

She dragged her guitar out to the field and sang to the corn and the crickets until the sun went down.

That night a
summer storm struck.
FLASH! went the lightning.
BOOM! BOOM!
sounded the thunder.
Baby Jacob began to cry.

"There, there," said Papa.
"Give the little fellow to
me." He bounced Baby
Jacob on one knee, but
it did no good.

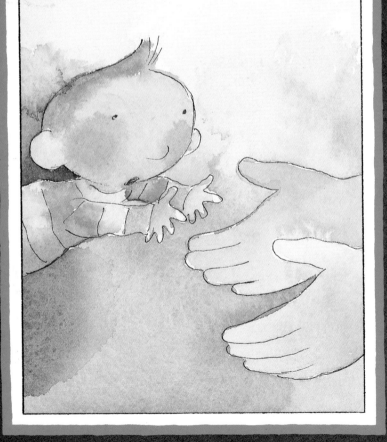

"Let me try," said Kate-Ellen.
She twirled Baby Jacob all
round the living room, but
he went on crying.

"I'll get him to stop," said Willy. He dangled a wiggly rubber worm in front of Baby Jacob's nose. But Baby Jacob cried louder than ever, *"WAAAAAA!"*

"I've got an idea," Sophie said. She took Baby Jacob into her arms. "Don't worry, Jacob."

She sat him in a chair and said, "That storm may be scary, but I'm not afraid." From the bottom of her heart, a song sang out – louder than thunder, stronger than lightning…

"I hate spinach!
I hate liver!
Last week I fell
into the river.
I bumped my knee,
I scratched my nose,
I lost my shoe, I tore my clothes.
Whenever trouble passes by,
I don't worry. I don't cry.

'Cos I'm a cowgirl, don't you see?
Yippee-ky-yuu!
Yippee-ky-yee!"

Baby Jacob giggled and clapped.
"He's smiling!" said Mama.
"He likes your song," said Papa.
"What a catchy tune!"
 said Kate-Ellen.
"Not bad!" added Willy.
"Will you sing another?"
 they all asked.

"Well, *jumping jack-rabbits*!" Sophie
said, strumming her guitar with glee.
"I thought you'd never ask!"

"Ducks and geese, they make me sneeze,
I have freckles on my knees.
I like jelly, mosquitoes like me,
I fell out of the big oak tree.
My ears are big,
my head is small,
It doesn't bother me at all.
I don't care!
Don't you know?

For Jaime, with a song in her heart
D. D.

To singing cowboys and cowgirls everywhere
R. L.

First published 1997 by Walker Books Ltd
87 Vauxhall Walk, London SE11 5HJ

This edition published 1998

2 4 6 8 10 9 7 5 3 1

This book has been typeset in Columbus MT.

Printed in Hong Kong

British Library Cataloguing in Publication Data
A catalogue record for this book is
available from the British Library.

ISBN 0-7445-5492-6